THE SCAM IN JUNIOR COLLEGE

AND

OTHER MYSTERY STORIES

RADHA SRINIVASAN MYSTERY SERIES

BY

YASHASWINI K

ISBN 978-93-5438-682-4

Published in India 2020 by Pencil

A brand of

One Point Six Technologies Pvt. Ltd.

123, Building J2, Shram Seva Premises,

Wadala Truck Terminal, Wadala (E)

Mumbai 400037, Maharashtra, INDIA

E connect@thepencilapp.com

W www.thepencilapp.com

DISCLAIMER: *The opinions expressed in this book are those of the authors and do not purport to reflect the views of the Publisher.*

AUTHOR BIOGRAPHY

Yashaswini K is a double post-graduate in Botany and English Literature. She is currently working as a senior journalist with vast experience in writing articles in the print and digital media.

CONTENTS

PREFACE

Shree Ganeshaya Namaha! To begin from the beginning, I have been discovering my creative side since my childhood. I had always loved a mysterious thriller that whetted my voracious appetite for reading. I even got a copy of a medical forensic science book from a library and got the entire book photocopied for my record! Writing murder mysteries came to me when I joined my undergraduate degree course in Science. A Post-Graduation in Botany gave the impetus to my creativity and when I became a journalist, I found a whole new world spread out in front of me to write about. Slowly, the concept of a crime reporter made my writing more credible and I conceived the character of Radha Srinivasan. 2019 saw me publishing the novel I don't want to meet Lord Krishna! which had this character Radha's encounter with the real Lord Krishna and the difficulties she faces due to that. One of the reviewers of the book asked me about this senior reporter's chemistry with Senior Inspector Keshav Pradhan. That prompted me to compile this book. This book consists of 6 different short stories, each consisting of different cases solved by Radha. I hope you will like them.

EPISODE 1. THE SCAM IN JUNIOR COLLEGE

I wrote this story in 2013 and think this is the right time to publish it with the other stories. This is also one of the stories I wrote based on a real incident:

It was November. Gauri Desai was returning home from the Acharya Kripa Junior College, where she was working as an English lecturer. She was definitely not in a humorous mood. On top of that a man was sitting on the bus seat that was reserved for women and was not ready to budge. After some argument when she turned to look at the conductor, the man commented, " You are weak so I have to leave this seat!"

Gauri realized that outsiders would not understand what she went through as a lecturer. People today took professionals in the teaching profession for granted. There was no place to sit in the class, with hardly any space for her to stand and teach. The whole place was hogged by more than 80 students. She had only the small platform to contend with. She even had to keep her books on the first bench. The authorities would say that teachers are not supposed to sit. Taking 4-5 lectures of 45 minutes each continuously was tiring. This included the proxy lectures of those who were absent on that day. Nobody bothered to understand that teachers are also human beings. Lecturers were often thrown out for no fault of theirs. The extra lectures of those dumped would also be thrown on her lap.

The moment the man got up and she got to sit, she called her mother and told her what had happened. She then angrily mentioned her problem. Her mother soothed her that at least she could get to sit after the argument.

The next day, it was Gauri's turn to be unceremoniously thrown out of the college, after serving them for 6 months, citing the excuse that she did not have class control. When she insisted one of the office staff gave her a hand-written experience certificate, with a lot of spelling mistakes. Besides, the certificate mentioned that she had worked for only 5 months. When she went to the principal and spoke to him about it, he said that there are a lot of issues. The teachers (he would call the lecturers as teachers!) did not pay the income tax, etc. But, he would definitely look into the matter. That she knew was an empty promise and the man was a sycophant, supporting whatever the owners of the college would do.

Gauri decided that to get justice, she had no other alternative than to contact Radha Srinivasan. Radha was her neighbor and a reporter in the newspaper The True Story.

"I don't understand when my salary is Rs. 4000 and only my profession tax is deducted, how they expect me to pay the income tax."

Radha looked thoughtful. She said, "Did you speak to the others? What do the others say?"

"They don't really care about it as long as they are paid some amount of money!"

Gauri continued, "In fact, the owner got a woman achiever award recently. She actually treats the teachers worse than dirt. To think of it, I find it ridiculous. The classroom is so stuffy. There is only one window. The students pay exorbitant fees but get benches made for primary school students. Though we are lecturers, the principal and the staff supervisor call us teachers and the students are encouraged to call us 'Miss'. Only the principal, staff supervisor and 2 other lecturers are already permanent to continue the scam for the owners. The 3-year contract system has become very convenient thing for them to continue their nefarious activities. Nobody is allowed to become permanent there. Otherwise they would have to pay everybody according to the pay commission directives. We were all finger-printed like criminals. And do you know what the man, who is the in charge of the teachers' lockers, said to me when I returned the keys. He asked me 'where is the lock?' when the lock is built into the locker. I felt so dirty," she looked disgusted.

"I am sure there is something fishy about everything out there. Ok. I need to speak to the editor and let me see what I can do."

The editor, Mr. Swaminathan Iyer, pondered over her query on how to expose the scam. He finally said, "Radha, you go try the English teacher's job. But I don't want you to go alone. Take Asha along. She can try the Physical Education teacher's job. Try not to get caught."

Asha Bhat was Radha's best friend and colleague. They had been together since their junior college.

During the interview, inside a small cabin within the staff room, which she later learned was the principal's cubicle, the Principal Mr. Bhattacharya clarified in the beginning itself to Radha, "The owners of junior colleges deposit their black money in the teachers' accounts, to make them white. Since you have not done B.Ed. you will get only Rs. 4000 from the deposited amount. You will not get the Christmas vacation payment. Even if we decide to continue you for the next year, you will not get paid for May vacations."

Luckily, she and Asha were immediately given the jobs. A male sports teacher was already present. Given the sheer number of students, a female sports teacher was also required. The junior college timings were noon to 6 in the evening. A Gujarati medium school functioned in the morning.

The next day the two newbies were taken to a nearby bank and savings account s were opened in their names. Radha asked the coordinator from the college if the passbook and cheque book would be given to her. He replied in the positive uneasily, looking at the bank officer.

When the cheque book came, Radha and Asha were made to sign on all the leaves of their respective cheque books. The principal explained, "If you are dumped, the other person, who comes in your place would still be paid from this account!"

Both Gauri and Radha had long hair and went to the same dance class to learn Bharatanatyam. Gauri had told her friend when she would wear her plaits in a particular way the students would tease her Chotiwali Miss behind her back. The other teachers complained to the Staff Supervisor Manpreet Kaur and the Supervisor in turn told her strictly not to wear her plaits in her classic way. Radha from day one wore her hair in the same way as Gauri as a challenge. The supervisor caught her after the first lecture and told her to leave her plaits loose.

"It is my hair and my decision. I will wear my hair the way I want. I am not your slave that I would follow your decisions about my personal things. If you have any problem with my work tell me I will rectify. Otherwise, please do not interfere with my personal preferences," Radha put her foot down.

After that, the teachers stayed away from her personal decisions. But, she knew they were looking for a chance to throw her out of the college like they did to Gauri.

The next day she and Asha were finger-printed the moment the principal came in for the day. The first day of her duty itself as a lecturer was difficult since she had to address more than 80 students in each class. So she asked the principal Mr. Bhattacharya, "Sir, it is difficult to speak very loudly in class. There are more than 80 students in every class. Can I have a mike?"

To that, the principal snapped, "How do the other teachers take lectures? If you don't know how to control the class, learn from them!"

Gauri had told Radha that some past lecturers from the college had lost their voice due to raising their voices above the din in the class. The next day, Radha was taking a lecture in the naughtiest class of XI std. Commerce and she had punished some boys, who had played mischief in her class. The other sports teacher Mr. Patil called her out and in front of all the students outside said, "The principal has said you should not punish the students by sending them outside the class. You don't know because you were not working here then."

"Oh, he said that, did he? I will comply with his order, if he tells that to me personally."

"If you punish them by sending them outside, it becomes a nuisance for those outside. Besides it does not look good in front of the people living in the surrounding buildings." The balcony was open towards the gate and could be seen from the residential buildings in the vicinity.

Asha was passing from there at that time. She came to Radha's rescue, "Sir, isn't Radha better equipped to deal with her class? Please let her do her job. Like she said if the principal has any objections with that he can talk to her. Do not create a problem for her in front of the students."

Radha finally asked, "Now, can I go back to my lecture?"

"If you want the principal to say it then he will," Mr. Patil actually stomped off in anger.

The principal never came!

At the end of the month, they all got payment in cash but they were made to sign on a register on which higher sums of money were written.

The next day, she had a class in XIth Science class, which was one of her favorite classes. She enjoyed teaching the Science class, perhaps because of her own Science background. She particularly loved the lesson, where a doctor lost all the fingers of his right hand due to a laboratory accident and regained it due to his research and some help by his own wife, who was also a doctor. The topic being right up their alley, the students listened to the lesson with pin-drop silence. After the lesson was over, the students came up with interesting questions.

"Miss, do you think this really can happen?"

"It could in future. Keep your minds open and be ready to accept what Science gives you."

Another student asked, "I read in the newspaper that a woman was given a kidney from a dead body. How can that be?"

"Yes, this is happening currently. It is called Cadaver Transplantation. The new kidney, if matches with the patient's body type, is transplanted."

A couple of days later, Radha had her dance exams. During break and free lectures in college she practiced while sitting on her seat, eyes closed in concentration. The supervisor told her to perform in front of them. The Commerce lecturer, Mr. Pitale, who was sitting in front of her, immediately commented, "Tell her to stand on the table and perform."

"Sir, this is Bharatanatyam not cabaret. There is a lot of difference between the two," was Radha's curt reply.

The only person, who would acknowledge her presence and respect her for being herself, was David, who taught Accounts. David sat right in front of her in the staff room. When they met outside, while entering the college premises, he would greet, "How are you Miss Radha Srinivasan?"

To which she would ask, "Hey, David, where is your Goliath?"

To which he would reply, "In the jungle."

They both had a very cordial relationship with each other. Radha felt very comfortable in his company, like she felt with her brother Kartik. That is why she would often call him David Bhaiya.

Radha had been sharing notes with Gauri regarding the happenings in college. Gauri had told her that one of the single female teachers Reena had tied rakhi to two of the male teachers one day before the festival. "But something is not right between her and one of the male lecturers Sudeep to whom she tied rakhi. Their whole attitude towards the brother-sister relationship is wrong."

One day, Radha found 2 students, a girl and a boy standing discreetly holding hands in front of their class. Before she could say anything, the Staff Supervisor, caught them and asked the boy tauntingly, "Is that your sister?" The boy immediately dropped the girl's hand.

After two lectures that day, when Radha was on her way to the ladies wash room, she saw Sudeep was walking towards the gents' wash room and Reena was returning from the ladies one. Sudeep stuck out his leg in front of Reena and she in turn pinched his buttocks. Everything happened in front of some students. So Radha warned Sudeep, "Can you keep these things private?"

After a few days fed up of the noise in some of the classes, while she taught the students, Radha spoke to the principal. She asked, "Is there a counselor in the college? I need to talk to her."

"Regarding what?"

"Sir, some students do not listen in class. When I take grammar class they say that they know it already so they do not want to listen. If they know it, why they don't perform well? So I need to talk to a counselor."

"So the gist of the matter is that you have still not got class control."

"Sir, with due respects, if I were a bad teacher then the 2 XIth Science classes would not be listening to me either.

Why do they listen to my lecture even if I take grammar? The problem is with the Commerce classes."

"There is no counselor here. Just concentrate on teaching better," the principal just brushed off her request.

The next day when she entered a XIth Commerce class, a disgusting sight greeted her. Written on the board was, "David loves Radha."

Revulsion consumed her and she left the class in a huff to the staff room. There she informed the staff supervisor about what she had seen. Manpreet's face turned red and she got up to come with her. In the class, the supervisor asked the students, "Who wrote this on the board?"

None of the students got up. Then, the supervisor turned to Radha, "You continue the lecture. I will find out who wrote it."

"Ma'am, I am not going to teach here unless the culprit is punished."

Right then David passed near them and looked into the classroom wondering about what had happened. He went into the classroom and spoke to the students. Within 5 minutes he had them apologizing to both David and Radha. The boy, who had written it on the board, came up to Radha and said, "I heard some lecturers link you both romantically, so I wrote it on the board."

Radha was very angry. She took the boy to the principal and told him what had happened. She then turned and looked at the supervisor, who had followed them into the principal's cabin. Even David had entered the cabin behind them. "I thought an education institute is a temple of learning. But this is what is happening in your college Sir." Radha said with aversion. "Unless and until I get a written apology from the culprit teachers, I will not teach."

The principal told the boy to go back to his class and told the supervisor, David and Radha to sit in front of him. Mr. Bhattacharya said, "I know that what has happened is wrong but you should not stop teaching."

"Then you won't even bother to find out which teachers are responsible for this? Do you know David Sir is like my brother?" Radha asked narrowing her eyes.

"Manpreet, do you know who the teachers are?"

"Sir, all this started some years ago when we realized that students of opposite gender had started dating each other. We started teasing them that they are brother and sister so that they would stop it."

"Is that the way you handle the situation?" Radha asked agitated. "What you started has taken such proportions."

The principal took a meeting, where he warned the supervisor and the other teachers not to continue teasing people about such things and he also told Radha to go on and teach, without asking the *teachers to give a written apology*. Radha realized that if she would be stubborn just then she would jeopardize her mission. So she left it at that.

The office assistant, Prabhakar Shinde was the in-charge of the lecturers' attendance. Gauri had told Radha that Prabhakar kept 2 attendance registers - one was rough, where they signed every day, with the time of arrival, while the other one was fair, which was for the record to be shown to the Exam Board. Since the time, she had joined the college; she kept her eyes open and watched Prabhakar when he was with the attendance registers. Finally, one day, she came early to college and saw him fish the rough one out of a cupboard in the principal's room.

That was the cue she wanted. She went out of the staff room and called her brother Inspector Kartik Srinivasan from her cell and told him about it.

The next morning after meticulous planning, Kartik and some female and male plain clothes persons from the police department, income tax department and the higher secondary examination board waited outside the college for Radha's signal. Radha could see Kartik, from the first floor window of the staff room. The teaching staff slowly trickled in and signed the rough attendance register. She knew that the accounts department would be working from the morning. She went to the window and held her cell to her ear. That was their signal. Every member of Kartik's group barged in through the gate. Kartik sent some of his men to the accounts department. Radha had already described to him the layout of the college, so it was easy for him to conduct the raid.

Radha on her part went and stood near the table where the rough attendance register was there. As Kartik entered the staffroom with some men and girls from his group, first thing that Radha did was to hand over the rough attendance register to him, to everybody's surprise.

Kartik's announcement further shocked them all. He said, "Nobody moves from their place. This is a raid."

Then 3-4 girls from his group went around collecting everybody's cell phones, including the principal's.

Mr. Bhattacharya stomped out of his cabin in anger asking, "What the hell is happening here? Who are you?"

"Mr. Bhattacharya, I am Inspector Kartik Srinivasan," he replied, showing his identity card. "Radha is my sister. We came to investigate a scam happening here. With me are the exam board and income tax authorities!"

"Anna, you can talk to some XIth std. students. I spoke to them discretely about the fees the college had taken. They not just take the fees, but also big amounts in the name of building fund donation. Please come to the class and have a look at the benches there. Given the exorbitant amounts taken as fees and donation, the students don't get any facilities."

After the classrooms were photographed as evidence, Kartik and Radha came back to the staff room. There they found the fair attendance register also, which he confiscated as well. On the ground floor, where the accounts department was present, they found two registers with records of the salary-rough and the fair ones. They also found the passbooks and cheque books in not only the name of the current staff, but also Gauri.

Kartik took the owner Razia Khan's phone number from the accounts staff and called her. When she arrived, she tried to bribe them and charges of bribery were also added to the charges against her.

EPISODE 2. THE STALKER

Radha Srinivasan got down from the rickshaw, hesitantly. The gates beckoned her with affection. She had always felt welcome at this place.

Senior Inspector Keshav Pradhan looked up from his desk as she entered his office. His eyes were soft and warm, but for a moment only, and the emotion disappeared as he spoke with determination. "No, Radha. I've told you time and again. I repeat, I won't reveal anything about this new case."

"This time I've come with something...well, personal."

"What could be... personal?" he asked asserting the last word. He looked mockingly at her.

"Look here, Keshav, I wouldn't be here if Kartik Anna were in town." Senior Inspector Kartik Srinivasan had gone to Delhi in search of a cybercriminal.

"Tell me what's wrong."

"I've been getting crank calls. Somehow, this guy knows when I am home..."

"Home? If I am not mistaken, you live in a hostel."

"I did. Our company felt it would be convenient if I and Asha live in their quarters closer to the office. That way we could be easily accessible."

"But, what's so dangerous or worrying about crank calls? It happens to most people particularly girls. At one time, even my sister used to get them. The trick is in how you handle them."

"'I like you, Baby' or 'Darling' is fine, but if the person starts stalking you, it's a different story."

"Hey, I thought you were a brave girl," his eyes mocked her again.

"There is a time for bravado. This is time to use common sense. See, if you want to help me, do it immediately. I don't have the time or inclination to be teased now."

"Gotcha! In your brother's absence, you can place yourself under my protection."

"Keshav, I can take care of myself. I just want to get my hands on that creep. Our landline did not have a caller id. We got it fixed, but it did not help. The man seems to be calling from different places at different times. He never calls on my cell. Asha convinced me that you will keep all this stuff under wraps."

"You seem to be in a rotten mood," he went on, relentlessly.

"You would be too if you were a girl and received this letter... It was dropped into our letter-box, probably during the night or early this morning," she put a sheaf of papers on his table.

The long letter that had been printed from a computer gave details of her whereabouts on all the days of the previous week with endearing punctuations. Time to time Keshav's expressions changed to one of displeasure while reading it.

"It is surprising that how much a stranger can know you just by observing you. Even I don't know so much about you," Keshav said seriously. "A stranger usually stalks a person to create fear or to blackmail the person. In your case, you being a crime reporter could be the reason."

"What do you mean?"

"You have helped the police place so many criminals in jail. One of them could have come out of jail and would be taking advantage of the fact that you are a girl. I will personally visit your home and handle the case myself."

Keshav came with her to their quarters, that evening and settled on the sofa in the hall and began glancing through a magazine.

"Do you plan to do something about my problem or just laze around here?" Radha asked, curtly.

"I have placed your landline as well as cellphones on surveillance. What else can I do now? Unless he calls, I cannot do anything."

As Asha brought coffee and snacks, she asked him, "Did you check on the criminals released recently?"

"Yes, I did." Keshav replied. "At least 5-6 of them had been sent to jail by Radha. They are being questioned right now. The letter is also being checked by our forensic experts. We hope we will know the outcome in a couple of days. But, I don't think we can get much out of it. Such criminals take a lot of care not to leave any tell-tale marks or fingerprints."

"I really wonder, who could it be," Asha looked thoughtfully at her coffee cup.

"You don't get these kind of calls, do you?" Keshav asked Asha.

"No, I don't. Why?"

"2 beautiful girls shift into a well-furnished flat in a residential complex. One girl suddenly starts getting crank calls. The other girl, doesn't. It does not add up."

"I have received a couple of blank calls, if that would help."

"So, whoever is calling wants to talk to Radha only. Now, who could be that secret admirer? Radha, do you know who could do such a thing?"

"No, I don't," she blurted. She picked up the coffee tray and said, "If I knew, I would have killed him by now."

She went to the kitchen to leave the tray there.

"She seems to be really upset," Keshav commented.

"Actually, it's you. You are upsetting her. Every time she has a tiff with you, she gets into such a mood."

"Really," he looked interested. "I never knew that."

"You don't know half the thing..."

At that time, the landline phone rang and both sat up. Radha calmly came out of the kitchen and picked up the receiver.

"It's for you," she held the receiver out for Keshav.

"Yeah..." Keshav was told by his deputies that 3 of the 6 criminals had been arrested and the questionings had begun. The other 3 could not be traced.

"So, it is one of those 3 criminals," Asha commented conclusively.

"Don't be so sure. But, I have told my officers to find as much information as possible about them."

"Could it be that any of the people still in jail are trying to scare Radha through someone else?" Asha suddenly suggested.

"It could be. My officers are also working on that angle, too. At the same time, Radha had rejected some suitors…"

"Who told you?" Radha's eyes opened wide.

"We do a thorough job always. Tell us more about the suitors."

"This person is NOT my suitor and I am NOT going to tell you about them."

"But, Radha, he seems to be a decent chap. What do you think?"

Radha looked at him for one second and turned away toward her room.

"You are leaving a blazing trail behind you. Your secret admirer might see it."

Radha did an about turn and said, "Keshav, gimme a break."

Before he could give another witty retort, the phone rang again.

Radha picked it up and spoke into it, casually. The moment she realized that it was her 'secret admirer' she signaled Keshav, who immediately became attentive.

Soon, Radha asked losing her patience "What do you want?"

"I want you," the caller replied. The next moment, she heard a clatter and a scuffle. Then, she heard a click and the phone went dead.

A few minutes later, Keshav got a call. He replied in monosyllables and hung up within minutes. After that, he told the girls that the stalker had been caught. It was already 2 AM, so he stayed back but told Radha to see him in the afternoon at the police station.

When Radha reached the police station, Keshav told her about the man, who had been stalking her. The man was a middle-aged divorcee and has become a psycho due to the breakup of his marriage. Keshav added, "Do you know, why he chose you over Asha? He said that you had a very innocent look on your face. He thought he could get a very good catch if he could marry you."

"Oh, I see. Is that all?" Radha asked, trying to be patient.

"Yes, that's it."

At that moment, his phone rang. "Yeah… Ok… Can we meet then?... She hung up."

When he had disconnected the call, he looked at her. She had a mischievous smile on her face.

He asked, "Do you know something about this call?"

"May be. May be not," she shrugged. Then getting angry, she added, "You, son of a …"

"Hey, hey, hey! Gimme a break," he imitated her.

"What break? I will break your bones," with that she got up and was about to approach him with vengeance, when he said, "Ok, ok. You win. I just wanted access to your home for a night. The owner of the house did not wait for our investigation to get over…"

"What investigation? There was no case from the beginning."

"There was. A woman was murdered in that house a few days before you shifted…."

"Why did nobody get to know about it?"

"Because the other reporters are not so nosy as you," he teased her.

"Stop it, Keshav. This is the limit!" Radha was angry. Saying that was an understatement. She was furious.

"Please sit down, Radha. I have not completed the story."

"Oh then, I am a child and you are telling me a story, right?" her eyes flashed in anger.

"Don't get me wrong. The owner of the house did not wait for our investigation to get over and had rented the flat to your company. We had only removed the seal on the house. I wanted to stay back for the night to search the hall where we had found the dead body."

"And why would that be?" she asked sarcastically. "That too after we shifted. Can you get any clues in the given situation? We could have inadvertently smudged the telltale marks."

"We had already got the preliminary investigations done. I had a suspicion that there was something we were missing. When I stayed overnight and you both had gone to sleep, I searched the wardrobe in the hall. I always wondered, why the wardrobe is in the hall. The owner of the flat said that it was not made by him. So, it turned out that it was made by the woman. I found a small secret chamber inside and there was the secret I wanted to find. The motive for murder – a diamond necklace. Now, I suspect someone and I just have to prove it."

"Now, who's that?"

"The husband of the woman, who went off and married his lover, as soon as he cremated his wife's body. I had an eye on him for some time."

"Now that your investigation is over, can I take leave of you, Sir?"

"Yes, you can."

"Good bye!"

He kept looking at the swinging door of his cabin long after she had left.

EPISODE 3. WHAT A WASTE!

It was the end of the working day. Radha Srinivasan was completely exhausted as she left the office. Hunger was striking cords in her belly. The vada pao stall beckoned invitingly. But, she wouldn't turn in that direction since she was on a diet. The ace journo of The True Story made her way toward the flyover, which would take her toward the other side of the railway tracks.

"Asha must have reached home and must have some warm scrumptious meal ready. Oh dear! My stomach is rumbling," Radha looked at the shops still open with inviting wafers and chocolates. She had to give them a pass since these were absolute no-no foods during dieting.

"Who's there on this side of the flyover?" Somebody was trying to get on this side of the incomplete parapet wall. She ran toward the shadowy figure. There was no streetlight nearby, she shined her pocket torch on the figure. She preferred the torch, though her mobile had one too. According to her, mobiles were meant for calling, messaging and the internet on the go. If she used it for the torch as well, then she might not have enough battery left till she reached home. If she got an emergency call? Or if she had to call someone, due to some urgent reason?

"Hey, what do you think you are doing?" The torch light revealed a man in his early 20s. Caught unawares, he straightened up.

"Why were you trying to jump on to the railway tracks?"

"It is none of your business, lady. Go home," the man was rude to her.

"No. I'll call the police, if you don't stop," she threatened.

"Who are you? A social worker?'

"No. I am just a citizen of this democracy…"

"Pooh, don't give me that crap about democracy. Democracy has gone to the dogs."

"Why do you say so?"

"Democracy cannot provide the necessities of life."

"How can you say that? You look like a decent young man probably educated. You might even have a roof over your head. What more do you want?"

"What else, but a job? Or that roof will not stay above my head. I have 3 more mouths to feed. This is the only decent pair of pants and shirt I have."

"Do tell me your story," she insisted compassionately.

"My name is Brahma Bhatt. I am a Brahmin. My father used to be proud of his Brahminhood. I say this with shame today. I had just completed my 10th standard when I lost my father. My distinction marks brought me scholarship for my further studies. Science fascinated me. I completed 12th standard amidst hardships. I had to earn, too. How much money could my mother's sewing bring in? As a result, I lost marks and could not make it to the merit list.

"Medicine posed another challenge. Neither did I belong to the reserved category not could I shell out the capitation fees, with my kind of marks. Finally, I opted to do B.Sc. in Chemistry. Today, nobody cares for graduates. People ask for additional qualifications in most places or experience. I had neither. Unless someone gives me a chance how can I prove my capabilities?

"One man, who had known my father put me up in his lab as a packaging boy. But, I couldn't keep that job.

"Why?"

"Is it my fault if I am a Brahmin? My name gives me away every time. Granted that Brahmins have tortured the scheduled caste people. But, that is old story. The reservation has avenged all the atrocities of Brahmins of the olden days had meted out to the lower castes."

"Yes," she agreed at that. "But, how does that connect with your losing the job?"

"My supervisor is a Buddhist!"

"Oh God, no," everything was falling into place now. Brahma Bhatt's superior had somehow thrown him out of the job just because he was a Brahmin. How nasty! This way a time would come that Brahmins would need to assert themselves and ask for a reserved category named after them. And all because some unseen ancestor of theirs had tortured some unseen ancestors of Harijans. And Mumbai claims to be cosmopolitan!

"Now, I don't have any other alternative than to commit suicide."

She just stared at him. This was not justified. Enmity handed down from generation to generation suited for Hindi films only. But, this kind of enmity against a whole community did not fit into the larger scheme of things in the present day and age. This kind of catching hold of victims when he is the most vulnerable reflected animalistic behaviour. "And I thought human beings are the most refined creatures," she thought.

Another thought struck her was Brahma Bhatt might be trying to gain sympathy and dupe her.

"What did he say was the reason for throwing you out of the job?"

"He says that I was there just for filling up a leave vacancy. The other person had returned, so I need to leave."

"And you don't believe it?"

"No, because my father's friend had told me that he had created a vacancy just for me."

"Did you speak to him?"

"No, I couldn't. He's gone out of town and will return the day after tomorrow."

"Does he know about it?"

"I don't know."

"How can you say that it is because of your caste that you were thrown out?"

"I have been working here for the last 6 days. Every day, I used to get a taunt about my caste. He even used to pass wisecracks about Brahmins."

"You could try elsewhere."

"I cannot try again from scratch. The house rent must be paid, today. My family have their daily requirements. My younger sisters need to go to school or at least they need clothing."

"Why don't you just change your name?"

"That would be worse than suicide. You can't help me, either. So, it's goodbye, then."

"What a way to go," I turned away helplessly brushing a tear off my cheek as I heard a big thud on the railway tracks and a train on the fast track coming in that direction.

The morning newspaper held the news about the suicide of a Brahma Bhatt at that same place. His face was smashed beyond recognition.

6 months later, Radha was asked to interview a pharmacist, who had made significant research toward curing AIDS. B Vishwanath looked oddly familiar. By the end of the interview, enlightenment dawned on her and he confidently

commented, "So you are a journalist. If you hadn't saved my life that day, I wouldn't have been able to achieve so much in so less time."

"Brahma Bhatt!?!" Radha almost shouted in astonishment. "Am I glad to see you alive! But, how did you…"

"To cut a long story short, I took the help of some friends to forge my certificates. Then, I applied for a job with faked experience in this private company. To change my appearance, I added a mustache and a beard. Most people do not cross-check the references since the candidates' competence reveals the experience and knowledge he has gained."

"Whose body was it then?"

"Before I could jump, a man came running and took a plunge. Then, the train smashed his face. He was a thief running away from a crowd. All I had to do was to change the identity of the dead body when no one was looking."

"And you achieved all this by faking your name and caste?"

"No, I don't have a caste now. I would prefer to be a human being."

"Incredible! After all, you are the same person and the competence is the same. What a sheer waste! If only you could have got it earlier, you need not have gone through all this. What a waste! Sheer waste!"

Footnote: 1. We were made by God as human beings and religions, castes and creeds are man-made. The varnas or castes were made for the smooth running of the society and not for any reservation.

2. Rules and laws need to be revised periodically.

EPISODE 4. THE AMNESIAC

"Hello," Radha spoke into the office phone.

"Hello? Is that Radha?"

"Who's this?"

"It's Keshav. Have you blocked my number on your cell phone? Your number is unreachable."

"You could have called me with a different name. Why did you give your real name?" She was still upset with him for playing a prank with her. "I don't want to talk to you," and she banged the phone down.

Within an hour, she was told to meet the editor in the conference room. Senior Inspector Keshav Pradhan was present there. Mr. Iyer told her to sit down near Keshav and said, "Aakash was found near the city dump under suspicious circumstances. He told the police that he worked here. But, he does not remember where he was for the last 48 hours. He is recuperating in the hospital, now. I want you to investigate this story with Keshav. First go and meet Aakash at the hospital. Ask Asha to come with you."

"Aakash, what were you doing near the city dump?" Radha asked Aakash. Asha was also present with her.

"I don't know, Radha," he looked perplexed.

"How come?"

"It's temporary loss of memory or amnesia," explained Keshav.

"Come on, Aakash. 2 days ago Mr. Iyer sends you to investigate a story and you end up near the dump. Something's really fishy."

There was no wound on his head, no concussion. But, Aakash could not remember any moment of the last 2 days when he had been investigating a case for *The True Story*.

"Now, wait a minute, Ms. Radha Srinivasan. What's this story all about?" Keshav demanded.

"Well, this is classified information," Radha said with attitude. *It was fun to watch Keshav tasting his own medicine!* "Speak to the editor. That's the way you usually work around problems," Radha turned her face away from the senior inspector.

The editor told Keshav that Aakash had been given a very dangerous assignment. He was investigating certain mysterious happenings in a place just outside the city limits near Thane district. It was near a resort that had come up recently.

Keshav communicated the information that the editor had told him to Radha and said, "I got a paper torn off from a letter-pad with their name, address and phone number from Aakash's pocket when we were searching him."

"Do you know something, I don't?" Radha demanded.

"Maybe. But, that is classified..."

"Then, why did you convince Mr. Iyer to tell me to join you in this investigation?" Radha was really offended this time.

"Hey, hey, hey. Guys, cool it," Asha tried to bring an order to the place. "We are here trying to find out what happened to Aakash, remember? So, there is nothing classified here."

"Near the resort is the Sethi Estate, a large mansion with a large compound surrounded by an electronically secured wire fence," Keshav gave in. "Last few months have seen some very suspicious happenings there. A couple of resort customers have seen murders happening in the mansion. *But, these customers themselves disappear before they can be questioned the second time!*"

Radha added for the benefit of Asha, "*The True Story* got involved when the resort owner, a very good friend of Mr. Iyer, asked my editor to send a reporter. Because of the lackadaisical attitude of the police department, he was on the verge of losing his business."

"Ma'am, only time will tell how lackadaisical the police department is. How would you like to investigate this story incognito and in partnership with a 'lackadaisical' member of the police department?"

"Who?"

"Yours truly."

"You?"

"Yes, me."

"And pray how will we be going incognito?"

"As husband and wife, to attract the least attention in our direction."

"Oh, no. I am out of it. I prefer to go with Asha, in that case."

"Radha," Asha said thoughtfully. "For once he is right. 2 girls would attract a lot of attention. But, nobody would bother a honeymooning couple. Besides, having a police officer around would beef up your security. And I'll always be just a phone call away."

"If you say so..."

"But, I will not stay with you in one room," Radha put her foot down.

"And attract everybody's attention? No, Ma'am," he seemed to be enjoying it. "But, you can take the bed. I'll take the couch, at night."

He had her in a bad position, but, she couldn't help it, could she? Radha had to get to the bottom of what had happened to Aakash. She had no other alternative than to comply with her companion's wishes.

"It's already dinner time," said Keshav looking at his watch. "After food, we will speak to the customers a little about the Sethi Estate."

Radha made a face and followed him to the dining hall. After a light dinner, they came to the lobby to go to the lawns when a familiar voice called Radha's name.

"Brahma Bhatt, what a pleasant surprise!"

"Radha, please remember I changed my name long time ago," he whispered to her.

"Ok. Vishwa. How's life?"

"It's going good. But, why don't you introduce me to your friend here?"

"I am Keshav," he extended his hand adding, "her husband."

"Satyanash!" Radha said in a loud whisper.

"Radha, you're married?" Vishwanath asked, quizzically. "I didn't know that."

"Me neither... I mean, I just got married. Keshav, will you please excuse me. I want to speak to Vishwa in private for a minute."

"Ok," Keshav said slowly looking at Vishwanath head to toe once. "Come back to the room afterward."

"Fine..."

"Shouldn't you be together? Or are you on a case, Radha?"

"Oh, nothing of the sort. I just want to be with you for some time. For a change. I have a few scientific questions for you," she looked around for a secluded place where nobody would hear them.

"Shoot, I am at your disposal."

"Vishwa, what does radiation do to our body?"

"Depends on what kind of radiation you are talking about. There are several types of radiation. UV radiation from sunlight in excess can cause skin cancer."

"I am talking about radiation from radioactive elements like uranium."

"Wow. That's it. I knew it. It has to be a case. You don't look like a married couple, too."

"Vishwa, please answer me. And don't talk anything about my marital status."

"Oh. That kind of radiation causes mutation in the cells of your body. There is no telling what direction these mutations can take. It could be cancer. It could cause a super-human being, anything. But, this depends on the period and the amount of exposure."

"Thanks, Vishwa. How long have you been here?"

"About 3 days, why?"

"Heard anything about the Sethi Estate, the estate adjoining this resort?" she waved her hand in that direction.

"Yeah. Suspicious things are happening there. Yesterday, I was passing near the compound wall, there when I heard somebody screaming and then a sound like some large thing had caught fire! What could it be?"

"I don't know. But, I sure like to find out."

"I want you to tell me what are you working on."

"No, I can't... Ok. Some days back an equipment was stolen from the army base in Kalina, Mumbai."

"And the equipment emits radiation?"

"Yeah, when Mr. Arora the resort owner told us about the mysterious happenings here, I figured..."

"So, you figured that Mr. Sethi had the equipment. You could very well have informed the police and asked them to storm the place."

"The police got involved since my senior, Aakash was found in a state of amnesia yesterday. Keshav is a Senior Inspector."

"I should have guessed it. Why don't you ask Keshav to get a search warrant to find out if the equipment is inside?"

"Well, actually," Radha revealed gleefully. "Keshav does not know the radiation thing! Besides, Mr. Iyer wanted us to get more concrete evidence before any offensive action is taken."

"You need my help anytime, I am here," he gave his room number, which turned out to be on her floor itself.

Radha walked thoughtfully toward her room. Could it be true that the equipment was on the Sethi mansion? Or could it be that something else was there which needed to be detected? Whatever it was, it was up to her...

"Ahh..." A blood-curdling scream rang out!

Radha ran to the balcony near her room overlooking the Sethi estate. The scream petered out into the sound of a large object starting to burn. There was light in the room directly in front of her. But, before she could understand what was happening a uniformed guard from the bungalow saw her and pulled the drapes to close the window. By then, Keshav had come out of their room and reached her. The others in their floor peeped out of their doors asking each other what had happened.

Radha told Keshav about what she had seen and heard. Keshav just looked her thoughtfully for a minute. They walked to their room, without uttering a word.

An hour later they emerged out of their room, wearing black. They stepped out of the compound of the resort stealthily and made a reconnoitering round of the Sethi Estate on the 3 sides other than the one adjacent to the resort.

The compound was bordered by a wire-fence, obviously electrically charged. Somehow, they needed to get in to find out what was happening inside.

While moving along the woods behind the mansion, Keshav found a dead pigeon. He was about to throw it away when he got an idea. Since he had gestured silence, Radha watched him tie its lifeless legs with a small but heavy stone. Then, like a shot-putter, he took an aim and threw it toward the fence. *As it hit the fence with a loud explosion, he pulled her down with him!*

All the lights in and around the mansion instantly went off. As Keshav pulled her up, and started running away from the point of impact, along the fence, she realized the reason behind this act. The only way they could get into the grounds was through the fence. But, the live fence could electrocute them. The only way the electric current could be cut at least for some time was by short-circuiting it.

As people ran toward the point of explosion, Keshav made her climb a large tamarind tree with sturdy branches hanging inside the compound. Once inside, Keshav started looking for a hideout. They found one before the lights came on again. Keshav pulled out a pocket torch and led the way into the mansion slowly.

There seemed to be nothing important on the ground and the first floors. On the second floor, the lights were on in the room opposite to where the stairs ended. There a group of about 6 guards was standing with a couple of other people.

One man was holding an equipment that looked like a dentist's drill. Keshav and Radha squatted near a couple of plastic drums, just outside the room, keeping an eye on what was going on inside.

The man holding the gun was laughing and saying, "This is the key to my success. Nobody will be able to control me, now. Ha ha ha. Sethi, you are a genius..."

Just then Keshav whispered her name and said, "Don't panic. There is a cockroach near you."

"Oh, it's only a cockroach." *When she turned, she saw that the cockroach was the size of a big rat!*

"Ye...," Keshav was in time to clamp her mouth shut. But, the commotion brought one of the guards outside. *He was the same man, who had seen her on the balcony of the resort, some time back!*

"Miss Radha Srinivasan, ace investigative reporter from *The True Story,* welcome. I also welcome Senior Inspector Keshav Pradhan, crime branch!" Sethi invited.

"How did you know my name?" Radha wanted to know.

"Oh. I know everything about you. Your friend Asha lives with you. Your brother is Inspector Kartik Srinivasan, Keshav's colleague. I even know where your parents are staying. Your colleague Aakash, wasn't that his name, was also on this case. He only got the laser, directed at the memory center of the brain. You will get the radioactive rays," his face turned hard. "I should have done the same with your colleague too. Then you would not have come here."

"On the contrary, we would have arrested you right away," Keshav spoke up calmly.

"On what charges? High speed radioactive rays do not leave any evidence, not even those which are left by fire. Whatever remains, I dispose off very neatly underground."

"What about the radioactive remains? You cannot shut them up permanently," Keshav spoke up.

"I dump them very far away from here and who can connect me to them."

"But, why, Mr. Sethi? Why all this?" Radha asked, curiosity taking the better of her.

"It's ok to tell you because you are going to die! I was a junior scientist with the army. I was brimming with ideas. I would suggest them to my seniors, but they would laugh it off as childish. Then, I heard that one of my colleagues had been promoted due to an idea he had picked up from me."

"I left the army and vowed revenge. The only way I could avenge myself was to develop a deadly weapon, through which I could take to task the whole nation. I had heard rumors that the army was planning to make a secret weapon. Snatching it from them was easy. I held the family of one of the junior scientists for ransom and the ransom was the blueprint of the weapon. From that I made this prototype," he said showing the drill.

"How do you contain the radioactivity?" Radha was still curious.

"The gun is made up of a similar but lighter material like the atomic power plants. Due to a secret process the electrons are made to travel 100 times faster than their normal radioactive speed. The result: every time I set this on R and press this button, the object in front of it burns with much higher intensity than with a normal fire and soon turns to ashes."

"But, I found out that your colleague was later thrown out of the army for the same reason, snatching of ideas," Keshav informed him.

"How did you know about this, Keshav?" Radha was surprised.

"We lackadaisical people also do some homework before setting out to investigate a case." Then, he turned to Sethi and asked, "Why are you directing your ire at innocent people? What did they do to you?"

"The army hasn't been punished. The officers, who used to taunt me have not been punished." "Enough talk. Girl come here. You will go first."

A guard pushed her toward the man, who was insanity incarnate.

"No," was all she could muster, struggling with the man. She knew she was done for. She looked for help toward Keshav, who was desperately struggling with 3 guards at the same time.

"Only a miracle can help us now," she thought.

Suddenly, a gun shot rang out and the radioactive gun fell from the injured hand of the mad scientist!

Radha turned with relief to see a police officer come into the room with Vishwanath and a hoard of constables.

"You, ok, Radha?" Keshav and Vishwanath asked her together.

"I am good. How did you get here, Vishwa?"

"I heard an explosion and came out to check. All the lights were out in this mansion. I went to your room, but, you were not in. I figured that you must be here and got the police. It turned out that we were just in time.”

“If there were nothing here?”

“But, Keshav, an explosion is an explosion.”

They all stood below an anti-radioactive shower to nullify the effects of radiation, if any. Before her turn came, Radha blurted, “Look at Sethi. He is the man, who directed his ire at the whole nation for what a few army officers did to him. And here is Vishwa, who decided to throw away his real name, get another identity and serve people. We need more people like Vishwa to strengthen our country by giving up their own identity!” With that Radha turned and marched off without realizing what she had done.

“...I owe her my life,” Vishwa said concluding his story. “But, I have told the owner of my company everything about my past. He was so impressed by my work that he disregarded my original identity.”

“If Radha thinks it is ok, it’s ok with me,” Keshav said, displaying implicit trust in her.

EPISODE 5. ITS AN ILL-WIND THAT BLOWS NOBODY ANY GOOD!

"But, Sir, why me? There are so many other reporters. Why me?" Radha Srinivasan asked.

"You are unique," My Iyer said.

"So? There are other people who are more unique than me."

"Radha no more arguments, please. This is my final decision."

"Ok, I give up!" and Radha stomped out of the editor's office in stubborn resignation. She was an investigative journalist working for the newspaper *The True Story*.

"Why the long face?" Asha questioned her as she came out.

"Perfect downsizing!"

"What do you mean?

"I have been transferred to the film desk!"

"What's downsizing got to do with it?

"Come on, Asha. Do you think there would be the kind of scope I have in crime reporting as a Bollywood reporter? All I'll have to do is chase the film stars and gossip about their private lives! Nothing else."

"You'll survive, dear," Asha said mock seriousness and then burst out laughing.

"It's easy for you to say that since you have been in the sports department since you joined this job. You love this job. You have not been shifted elsewhere all through this time. I joined this publication much later, only about 2 years ago and I am being shifted! I want to resign, but I want to be self-sufficient and independent and this is the only way I know."

"Come on Radha, be a sport. I'm sure you will do fine as the entertainment reporter. If not, we'll all request Editor Sir to transfer you back."

"Ok," she sighed listlessly.

Radha's first assignment as the Bollywood reporter was to interview an upcoming cinematographer, Syed Raza. Radha tried to put her mind to the task in hand, unwillingly and decided that whatever she had to do she would do with the same enthusiasm as she did before. Therefore, she requested the cinematographer over the phone that she would meet him on the sets to understand his work enough to be able to do justice to his interview.

The day was overcast when she reached the sets at Kamal Amrohi studios. The set designer, who had constructed the sets, was an upwardly mobile person. The sets themselves were fascinating replicas of the real thing. Only keen observation on her part would let her distinguish between fakes and the genuine structures.

After exchanging pleasantries with Syed, she watched him take aerial crane shots till lunch time. Declining to lunch with him, she roamed about the whole area observing interestedly every aspect of the set and its building. At one point, she watched as a man carried the camera to a room, closing the door behind him.

Radha did not think much of it and returned to the place where Syed had promised to be waiting.

"Where does the camera go after the shooting?" Radha asked at the end of the interview.

"They go to the editing studio for processing with the software Premier Pro CC. Would you like a sneak peek into those processes? Luckily, I am going there, too, right now. Would you like to join me there?"

"Sure thing. I wouldn't give up such an opportunity. I would like to apologize to you to you and your kindred. I was transferred only today from the crime desk and thought that I would only be chasing film stars and writing gossips about their private lives. Now that I am into this, I find that there is more to films that meets the eye."

"You are right. Films are not just stars performing on screen. A lot of technical work goes into the making of every film. Things have become easier in the digital age."

"The memory cards are all blank, Syed!" the video editor came out of the lab with the disappointing news. "Nothing is present in them!"

Radha could sniff the fragrance of a crime right away and turned to her interviewee with anticipation. Syed's face was downcast. "We'll have to go through everything again, then. This was the last schedule. Getting star-dates is a big problem for the producer. I'll be held responsible for this. I am at the threshold of a promising career..."

Radha was moved. She put herself into his position and thought that if it were one of her articles that had been sabotaged, instead? God-forbid, it had never occurred till then. The True Story staff including the editor, Mr. Iyer had been like a family.

"Do you have any enemies?" was the first question that popped into her mind.

"No," was the monosyllable reply.

"Do you know anybody who could go to any extent to sabotage your career?"

"No."

Radha's gut feeling insisted that Syed was hiding something, probably since she was basically a crime reporter, so she thought she ought to set things straight.

"Syed, I'm talking very honestly, man to man. If you think I will use this against you, be rest assured I won't. I only want to help you. I won't publish anything until we get to the bottom of this and catch the real culprit."

"Do you promise me that? But, how can I trust a journalist?"

"You can trust me. Look here, I will not breathe a word about this incident even to the film editor. I will only file the interview. Now, do you trust me or do I give it in writing?"

"That's ok, I trust you. There is someone, who would be interested in damaging my career, but I don't know who it is."

"Some other cinematographer?"

"Dunno…"

"Ok. Were there, really, quite a few contenders for this job as you said earlier in the interview?"

"That I had exaggerated a bit." He replied sheepishly. "But, there were a couple of other technicians vying for the job."

"Who are they?"

Syed gave her a couple of names. "But, they are my friends and they are out of town today. I don't think they…"

"Someone else might have done it on their behalf. Actually, I think I saw it happen right in front of my eyes!"

"What exactly happened?"

"Yes. During lunch break, I saw…" She narrated the incident where the camera was taken into a room.

"That is nothing. My assistant was just taking the camera to that room and he was just keeping it in his safe custody. He is a very trusted friend of mine. He couldn't have done it. According to what the video editor said, I think it must have happened on the way here or during the time the interview was going on."

"Are you absolutely sure?" Radha still doubted the young assistant. "How did you get the indication that someone was trying to sabotage your career?"

"Couple of telephonic warnings against my doing this film and a camera was destroyed in an out-door schedule.

Syed promised to keep her posted on the developments and they parted ways. Radha on her part made discreet enquiries with her film editor about the other two cameramen, who did not get the job and drew a blank. Before the editor could get suspicious about her questioning, Radha went to her desk to file her report. All through the evening, her mind was on who would have erased the memory card.

Radha was about to leave the office, with Asha, that night when she got a call from Syed. Both the girls stayed in the same hostel. He sounded agitated. "Somebody is seriously interested in stopping me from doing this film. Radha, this time it is a computer printed message left inside my house.

"Inside the house? Was it broken into?" she asked.

"No, that's the most surprising thing."

Radha and Asha reached his house in an hour's time. By then, Syed was almost hysterical. He wouldn't care less about Asha being there. Syed lived alone in the third floor flat of Millat Manor in Jogeshwari West.

"Obviously, the person knows you and has a key to your place," Asha observed, looking at the letter.

"Then how else can the message land on the dining table located in the kitchen on the opposite side to the door, like you say it did? The window wasn't open, was it?" Radha was, by the minute getting suspicious of Syed, himself. Some people from the Hindi filmdom would play any kind of publicity stunt to get recognition, she'd heard.

"No," he replied.

The girls left Syed's home and caught a rickshaw to their hostel.

Once inside their room, Asha observed that her friend was thoughtful and asked her what was wrong. Radha told her about her suspicions about Syed.

Asha tried to put her doubts to rest. "But could he go to the extent of damaging his work to do that?"

"He could, if it's a team-work. Don't you remember cricketers have manipulated the ball to win a match?"

"That maybe, but I feel, Syed is Ok."

"Only this letter that I took from him will tell. There was no printer or computer or laptop for that matter in his house. That doesn't mean he hasn't hidden it somewhere else or used someone else's device on the sly. The most accessible offices to these technicians are usually the producer's equipment, whose movies they are working on. First thing tomorrow morning, we'll have to make rounds of those offices and check out the computers and the stationary papers."

The next day, Syed met Radha and Asha in their office. Radha had invited him there. "How will you know the difference in the papers?" Syed was perplexed. "If they were typewritten papers, then an expert could have found the difference. These are computer stationary."

"Radha, are you thinking what I'm thinking?"

"I think so, sweet heart. There are so many fonts available in the software market and they can be used by anybody anywhere. There wouldn't be any luck with the handwriting since it has not been signed. But most big companies often have their own watermark on their papers. We need to compare their executive bond papers with the paper used to send the warning. I saw a water mark on it. The question is how to get the stationary."

Both the girls slowly turned to Syed.

"No, I can't do it. I might get caught," Syed protested.

"But, you are the one who has access to these offices," Radha tried to persuade him. After some more amount of convincing, he reluctantly agreed.

As the girls saw Syed leaving their office, Asha asked thoughtfully. "If Syed doesn't get the papers, then?"

"By then I'll have something else up my sleeve." Radha replied determinedly.

Syed had discreetly brought some executive bond papers from different film company offices for whom he had been working. In one corner of each of the papers, he had written the name of the company from where he had got the papers.

Later when they compared the bond papers to the warning note, they drew a blank. So, she thought, if Syed had done it, it would have been with some other company's paper or someone else was behind it.

"But, the paper could have come even from a cyber café or any other stationary store," Syed suggested.

"Syed, when you say that bond paper is available in cyber cafés and stationary stores, the paper will be unique to the company, which manufactures it. I've seen the other common stationary with watermark. This is different, unique to a particular company or some individual, who can afford to get many of these papers in bulk."

" That is where the cookie crumbles. There could be so many people out there, who have such papers with them and we cannot find them. The only way we can do anything is to find my brother, Senior Inspector Kartik," Radha replied helplessly.

The next day, Asha left for office and Radha was on her way to find her brother. When she was about to enter the police station under the charge of Kartik, she got a call on her mobile. It was Asha. "The Entertainment editor is furious, yaar. Come on here immediately. Something has come up," Asha sounded very excited.

"Where were you, dear? You have to get an important story done," Shalini Jukar, the film desk editor, told her.

"You have to meet upcoming writer, Gaznavi, today. I suspect that his latest story has been lifted by someone. It is not clear who. The appointment has been already fixed for you. Try to make him speak about the episode, since he had last month gone to print about his landmark story," were her instructions.

According to her background research, Gaznavi was a young writer, who had given a few hit films. However, critics were not happy with him since there was no originality in his work, according to them. The story, about which her editor was talking, had been a very original work, an effort he had been trying to make since the start of his career.

When she reached Gaznavi's house, he was typing something on a laptop.

"Do you type your stories, usually?"

"Yes. Would you like to see the scene I'm writing?" Gaznavi offered.

"Thanks," she replied and found him typing in Verdana font, the point size very like that of the note Syed had received!

Though the point size of the letter seemed like the story being typed by Gaznavi, that did not say that he was the culprit. But, he was, definitely, one of the suspects. However, it was not clear, why would he try to destroy Syed's career.

At the end of the interview, Radha asked a couple of questions about taking the print-out of his story for going ahead with the movie-making process. Gaznavi was in the seventh heaven, having given a good interview. Thus, he obliged. He even gave her a message for his fans in the form of a print-out.

He had declined to comment on the lifting of his story, but, had said cryptically that the culprit would suffer. This comment and the matching of the print-outs were leading to the formation of an idea in her mind. But, she needed further proof.

Radha's sensitive reporter's nose took her back to the sets in Kamalisthan where the last few shots were being shot again. She asked Syed to give her a couple of minutes and he obliged. Radha told him her theory that perhaps Gaznavi was behind the accidents on the sets of Syed's movie.

"It can't be. We've known each other since childhood. We are very good friends even now. He wouldn't do anything like that."

"Did you know that his story has been lifted by someone and I suspect that the movie being made is this one."

"What? I can't believe it."

"If not, what is the connection? Ok. Tell me, are the other technicians being threatened, in a similar way?"

"Not that I know of. But, you can speak to the director."

As soon as the director had given a negative reply, a car came straight for them!

Syed pulled Radha away from its path and the director jumped to the other side. They all turned to see it crash onto a large part of the sets. The man inside was completely haggard and was hurt at several parts of his body.

"Producer Sahab, what happened?" Everybody ran toward the man.

"The brakes failed," he replied, limping on his right leg toward a chair.

Producer Malkani was a builder, who was investing in an Indie film for the first time. He spoke at length to Radha about his film and the events that were taking place during the shooting. He said that he had received threatening calls and a couple of notes. The latter he had destroyed since he thought they meant nothing to him. Radha also put forward her theory of sabotage without going into details on who was behind it.

"I know, who is behind it. The underworld!" replied Malkani. "I thwarted their attempts to drain my bank balance…"

At that moment, his mobile rang. He excused himself, shouting into it; he limped on his left leg. Radha went to the car before the mechanic could reach the place and looked into it, to find what she wanted. The maximum damage had occurred to only that side of the sets.

Radha found out the name of the writer of the movie, Kazi and went to meet him to ascertain if he had actually lifted Gaznavi's story. If he had, Kazi did not give an indication of it. About the events occurring during the shooting, he was aware of it only by way of what he had heard from people. This was because he would rarely go to the shoot. It also meant that he had not been sent any of the warnings.

"That is odd," Radha thought. "If Kazi has lifted Gaznavi's story, then Kazi should have been the main target. Why is Gaznavi trying to sabotage his good friend Syed's career by damaging the sets and tamper with the memory cards? Obviously, Gaznavi is not the real culprit! I was on the wrong track, then. So, the main motive behind these incidents were not to sabotage anybody's career. But then, why were they happening? If disruption of the shoot was the main aim, then why were the incidents not happening every day and why did they not happen when the first schedule began? These incidents were more recent. And why were the other technicians not affected by the incidents? Why only Syed?

Then, there was something else, in fact, 2 things that happened the day the producer's car crashed onto his movie sets. They did not fall into place - something she saw inside the car and the producer's behavior. What were they? She could not remember.

She had peeped into the car to confirm that the brakes had really failed. But, she had seen something else, too. What was it? Yes. The handbrakes were in working condition.

Then, why hadn't Malkani used them? And then why did he first limp on his right leg and then left?"

Everything was so confusing!

At that time, her mobile rang. It was Syed. "Gaznavi's story was not lifted by Kazi. A big banner writer-director had lifted his story and the shooting had already begun in Switzerland. And Gaznavi did not mean anything mean by talking about the culprit suffering. He meant he is going into direction himself and intends to complete the film before the other one," Syed informed.

"Syed can you meet me at our newspaper office in an hour's time, please? I think I'll have enough information by then about the happenings," she requested.

An hour later, Radha had an interesting story to tell. A man came to Mumbai from Punjab in the 1980s. He hailed from a family predominantly into business. They were suffering from heavy losses due to the terrorism prevalent in those days. The man wanted to make good those losses in the city of opportunities. He first became a building contractor and within 10 years due to various scams that he had done, became a builder. With quite a few builders taking to film-making, he signed a hit director 2 years ago to make a movie. All the other technicians were novices. Some months back he found that the director was delaying the project unnecessarily and demanding more money. Therefore, the producer went on to insure all his equipment, including the sets that were built against accident.

Any kind of accidental damage to the equipment or set structure before all the schedules got completed, would ensure him of easy money.

Malkani knew that threatening the director would not work and would point fingers at him only since everyone was witness to their argument about the pay hike. On the other hand, threatening other technicians would be ineffective. He could not stop the shooting since he had already invested a lot of money into the movie.

Anonymous threats to Syed would make him stop shooting out of fear. The next cinematographer, who again would have been a newcomer would be threatened. This would go on and somehow the shooting would be completed. This was his plan. But, Radha came to interview Syed and she happened to visit the laboratory to begin her investigations.

"But, I haven't understood how and why he framed Gaznavi and dropped the letter in your house?"

"That was easy. The 3 of us knew each other very well for the last 5 years. He could get the keys to both our houses at the drop of a hat. Gaznavi could be framed easily due to his plagiarized story."

"You did not say this to me before?"

"I never thought that Malkani could do such a thing. How did you find out?"

"An idea, a couple of calls to the different insurance companies and the director of your film. I took my brother Kartik's help wherever I could not access any information."

"What will happen to him?"

"My brother has informed the specific insurance company about the scam. When he goes to them with a claim, they will take care of it. Whatever he did boomeranged on his face."

Asha said, "Yeah, It's an ill-wind that blows nobody any good!"

EPISODE 6. THE PASSING OF A LEGEND!

Radha Srinivasan entered *The True Story* office and was told to visit the editor's central cubicle in the editorial department, immediately. The editor, Mr. Iyer told her to pull up a chair close to him. With him was Katherine D'Costa, the Bollywood reporter. Katherine or Kates, as Radha called her, was a good friend of hers.

The editor told Katherine, "Go ahead and tell her what you told me."

Katherine said, "Your favorite female actor Prakriti was found dead in a little known resort in Goa this morning."

Radha looked at her friend, shocked. The next moment, she shook herself and asked, "Are you sure?"

The editor gestured the girls to lower their voices. She continued in a low voice, "The whole incident is a little fishy. I suspect foul play."

Radha asked her in a low voice, "How do you say that?"

Katherine explained her suspicions and asked her, "I requested Iyer Sir to ask you to investigate. I will help you with anything you need."

Mr. Iyer said, "You can go and investigate the case, immediately. Take Asha Bhat along with you. Be ready to stay there for at least one week. Constantly, keep in touch with me through my private number and email."

As decided, the 3 girls left for Goa on a flight 2 days later. They were following all the information being given on the TV channels regarding the sad news. When the flight was in the air and the sign of wearing seatbelts was switched off by the cabin crew, a man came toward the girls.

Radha saw him and exclaimed excitedly, "Anna? What are you doing here?"

The man in front of the girls was Radha's elder brother Inspector Kartik Srinivasan. With him was Senior Inspector Keshav Pradhan. They were in plain clothes. Radha looked away from Keshav because she was still angry with him for playing a prank with her. Kartik looked at his sister smiling and said, "Surprise! We are here for the same purpose as you. Mr. Iyer told us to join you."

Radha introduced her brother to Katherine and Kartik introduced his colleague to Katherine. Kartik did not say anything further and both the police officers sat on the empty seats across the aisle.

The girls began talking in low voices about the case. At that time, Asha said, "We will have to wait till we land to talk to Kartik Anna and Keshav for more information."

At Dabolim Airport, they all deboarded the flight. The fivesome made it to Stevenson Beach Resort in Polem, soon and booked 2 rooms for themselves. Then, the men came to the girls' room to discuss the further course of action in the case. They carried the chair from their room with them. There was one chair already present in the girls' room. The men sat on the chairs and the girls on the bed.

Radha began, "Let's list the known facts about the case. First, Actor Prakriti is found dead in the bathroom of one of the rooms at this resort. Prakriti is or was a South Indian actor working in Bollywood movies. Second, she seems to have drowned in the bathtub filled with water."

Asha took up from there, "Third, there was a small but significant gash on the back of her head. Fourth, traces of alcohol were found in her blood. Fact remains that Prakriti did not drink hard liquor. Fifth, she was a very healthy person. These last 2 facts do not add up, with the rest. Do we know anything else?"

Katherine spoke up, "Prakriti was at the peak of her career. There were rumors of her marriage with someone from the industry, some years ago. We don't know who. The dead body's photograph given to the reporters looked different from Prakriti. That made me suspicious."

Keshav joined the discussion. He said, "I know who she was married to."

Everybody turned to look at him. He continued, "He is a movie producer named Manav Singh Rajput. They were divorced recently."

"How did you know?" Radha asked Keshav Pradhan.

"I have been doing some background research on this case from the time reports of her death began to be circulated around. I knew Radha would be assigned the case and Mr. Iyer would ask us to investigate it with her. Mr. Iyer has also told us to investigate the case incognito and not to go to the local police."

"Why did our editor tell us to investigate the case incognito? And how did we journalists not know about the marriage and divorce?" Radha wanted to know.

"Mr. Iyer has his own reasons. The matters of Prakriti's marriage and divorce were hushed up," Keshav replied.

"So, what else do we know?" Asha asked.

Kartik replied, "At the moment, the local police have sealed the entire floor where the death took place."

"So now, it is the time to find out more," Asha voiced everybody's thoughts.

That night it was decided that they would go to the third floor room where Prakriti's body was found and investigate further. They had already had a light dinner at the dining hall on the ground floor. The girls went first trying to behave casually. The men followed them making sure no one saw them. On the third floor, there was nobody keeping a watch. So, the fivesome carefully passed the police-made barriers and moved toward the room where the deceased actor was staying before she died.

They were about to reach the room where Prakriti was staying before her death, when Asha detected some movement from the direction of the service lift. The fivesome began to look for a hideout. They found the storeroom, which was not locked. They went into the small room. The space was cramped. But, they managed to squeeze inside. Keshav opened the door just a crack and he saw a room-boy pass them with a trolley having covered food-filled dishes on it. The fivesome could smell the delicious aroma of the food from their hideout.

Keshav immediately closed the door carefully. When he opened it again, the room-boy was not to be seen. The fivesome came out of hiding. Kartik asked, "This floor is sealed. Nobody is supposed to be here. Where is this room-boy taking the food?"

The fivesome looked around, again and still could not see the room-boy. So, they advanced toward the room where Prakriti was staying on the fateful day. Keshav fished out a Swiss knife and tried to open the built-in lock of the door. Initially, it did not budge. But minutes later, it opened silently. They entered and closed the door behind it, just in case they were found by someone. They searched the room. But, none of them came up with anything. It appeared that the police had made a thorough search.

This time Katherine heard someone outside the room. The knob turned and the fivesome ran helter-skelter looking for places to hide. It was the room-boy. The young man looked around in suspicion, went out and closed the door. The fivesome came out of hiding and found themselves locked inside the room.

"Now what?" Radha asked.

"Now, we go out before the room-boy brings someone with him," Keshav replied and went toward the door. Using the Swiss knife, he opened the door again from the inside. When they walked out, they heard 2 men talking to each other. The sounds were coming from the direction of the service lift. Keshav directed all the others toward the storeroom. They were just in time to close the door as the room-boy and the manager passed them to go to the room they were in, some time ago. When they went inside the room, Keshav gestured the others to leave together. When the fivesome were out of earshot of the manager and the room-boy, they gave out sighs of relief. They reached the girls' room and discussed the developments behind closed doors.

"Something suspicious is really happening here," Radha commented. "There is someone on the floor where no one is supposed to be."

"What can be the right course of action now?" Asha asked.

"Though things are suspicious here, we are looking for evidence in the Prakriti case. And that will be hindered if we go looking for the hidden person," Katherine observed.

"On the contrary, I would rather we look for the hidden person. Who knows, we might find something significant,"

Kartik suggested. "Come on. There's no time to lose. We have to go back before they shift the hidden person to a different place."

They all freshened up and made another trip to the third floor. This time there was a room-boy, sitting on a chair, near the staircase, overlooking the lift, as well. Kartik disabled him and the fivesome went further. There was no one else on the lookout on the floor. Keshav had to open each door to make sure they did not miss anything. Further down the corridor, as he tried to turn the lock with the Swiss knife, they heard a muffled sound from inside the room. Keshav gestured the others for silence and opened the door. A stench of urine mixed with fecal matter greeted them.

When their eyes got used to the darkness, the fivesome saw a figure uncomfortably tied to a chair inside the room!

The girls ran toward the frightened woman and at closer look the rescuers were shocked. *The woman was Bollywood actor Prakriti!*

When the girls tried to touch Prakriti, who had been beaten black and blue; the actor cringed away from them, in fright. Then, she recognized Katherine and Radha and began to cry, loudly. Keshav requested her not to cry aloud and she began to calm down.

Radha undid the ropes that held her. Asha removed her gag and gave the hapless lady some water from a bottle, which was lying nearby. Prakriti told them, "I was returning home from a shoot here and Manav kidnapped me, a few days back. I have lost track of the days. He wants my wealth and property. He has been torturing me all this while. The local police are also with him. This resort is his benaami (in someone else's name) property."

Right then, the door-knob turned and Manav Singh Rajput came in with the manager and some room-boys. The room-lights were also switched on. He uttered, "Welcome, Friends. When the manager told me that we had some interesting guests, I realized that someone had come trying to look for Prakriti."

"And you had that room-boy watching the way to this floor," Keshav spoke up.

"Yes," he replied, sneering. "Senior Inspector Keshav, you are smart. But, you will not be able to leave here."

"Whose dead body's photograph did you show to the press?" Katherine wanted to know.

"That was just a photoshopped image. We wanted to take Prakriti's photograph like a dead body. Prakriti did not cooperate with us. Enough talk. Boys, tie them up!"

But, before the room-boys could do anything, the room was flooded with army commandoes. The leader ordered, "This resort has been surrounded. You have no other alternative than to surrender."

Realizing that their game was up, all the criminals surrendered and were herded out, together. In the commotion, the girls helped Prakriti up from her chair. She got up weakly. The fivesome triumphantly walked out of the room with the celebrity, they loved.

Radha called the editor, happily, the moment they reached the girl's room, "Sir, we found Prakriti Ma'am."

Mr. Iyer replied, "I knew you would. I had a suspicion about the local police. That is why I requested the police commissioner to send Keshav and Kartik with you."

"Sir, did you ask the army to intervene as well?"

"No, I did not," he replied surprised.

When the call was over, Radha asked, "But, I have still not understood, how the army commandoes arrived at the nick of time."

Keshav spoke up, "It was an arrangement we had with the army. The police commissioner of Mumbai had contacted the high command of the army and it was decided that we would have a joint operation."

Kartik added, "Manav is not only involved in Prakriti Ma'am's kidnapping. He has an illegal drugs and arms business going on from here. He also has a strong connection with the underworld."

"I still wonder how he had fooled the entire world about Prakriti Ma'am's death with that photoshopped image!" Radha said thoughtfully.

"The fact remains that he could not fool Katherine," Asha told her, smiling.

Prakriti had by then freshened up and was wearing Radha's clothes. She thanked the fivesome for rescuing her.